Power Pitchers

By Jim Gigliotti

The
Child's
World®

www.childsworld.com

Published in the United States of America by The Child's World®
1980 Lookout Drive • Mankato, MN 56003-1705
800-599-READ • www.childsworld.com

ACKNOWLEDGMENTS

The Child's World® : Mary Berendes, Publishing Director

Produced by Shoreline Publishing Group LLC
President / Editorial Director: James Buckley, Jr.
Designer: Tom Carling, carlingdesign.com
Cover Design: Slimfilms

Photo Credits
Cover–Robbins Photography
Interior–All by Robbins Photography except Getty Images: 7, 8.

LIBRARY OF CONGRESS CATALOG-IN-PUBLICATION DATA

Gigliotti, Jim.
  Power pitchers / by Jim Gigliotti.
     p. cm. — (Reading rocks!)
  Includes index.
  ISBN-13: 978-1-59296-860-2 (library bound : alk. paper)
  ISBN-10: 1-59296-860-0 (library bound : alk. paper)
  1. Pitching (Baseball)—Juvenile literature. I. Title. II. Series.

GV871.G56 2007
796.357'22—dc22

                              2007004204

CONTENTS

THE
Lefties

Major League pitchers come in all shapes and sizes. Some are tall, like 6-foot 10-inch (180 cm) Randy Johnson. Some are short, like 5-foot 7-inch (147 cm) Fabio Castro. Some are as big as football players, and some are rail-thin. There are 40-year-olds and 20-year-olds.

Their talents are as different as their sizes and ages. Some get batters out with a blazing fastball. Others rely on their **curveball** or **changeup**. But all great pitchers have some things in common.

They all have focus and determination. They are confident in their abilities. They know which pitch works best for them, and they use it to get the big outs.

Let's meet some of the best pitchers in the Major Leagues. We'll start with the lefthanders, who are sometimes called "southpaws." Many experts consider the Minnesota Twins' Johan Santana to be the best pitcher—from either side—in the game today.

Is lefty Johan Santana the best pitcher in baseball?

Santana's best skill is his ability to throw several types of pitches for strikes.

Santana can blow the ball past opposing batters with his fastball or fool them with his changeup. Plus, he can throw whichever pitch he chooses to the location he wants.

Earned run average (ERA) measures how many runs a pitcher allows in nine innings.

In 2006, Johan won the American League's **Cy Young Award** for the second time in three years. He led the AL in wins, strikeouts, and **ERA** (earned run average).

Johan has succeeded Randy
Johnson as baseball's most
dominant left-hander. Randy
returned to the Arizona
Diamondbacks in 2007 after
playing for the New York Yankees
in 2005 and 2006. The big lefty just
might be the scariest pitcher ever.
He towers over almost any hitter,
and when he stands on the mound,
he looks even bigger!

Johnson will scare NL hitters in 2007 with Arizona.

Even scarier is his 100 mph
(161 kph) fastball. It's not
surprising that Randy has
struck out more batters
than anyone else in
baseball history—
except for Hall of Fame
pitcher Nolan Ryan.

Barry Zito moved to the NL when he joined the Giants in 2007.

Unlike Randy Johnson, Barry Zito doesn't rely on an overpowering fastball to get hitters out. Instead, his best pitch is a nasty curveball. Batters know Barry is going to throw them his curveball, but they still aren't ready for it! That's why Barry won 102 games for Oakland from 2000 to 2006. He won the 2003 AL Cy Young Award. In 2007, Barry became the highest-paid pitcher in Major League history. The lefty switched teams for 2007, signing a contract with the San Francisco Giants worth $126 million.

One of Barry's teammates on the A's was Mark Mulder, another young lefty. Mark has a "sneaky" fastball. That means it's faster than hitters think it's going to be from watching his **delivery**.

Mark Mulder won at least 15 games for five seasons in a row.

Mark, who now pitches for the St. Louis Cardinals, was slowed by injuries in 2006. But the Cardinals signed him to a new contract for 2007 because they think he'll be back in top form again.

Tom Glavine is a lefty who always seems to be in top form. The New York Mets' star turned 40 years old in 2006, but he's still one of the best southpaws in baseball.

Like many good pitchers, Tom has **adapted** over the years. He doesn't throw the ball as hard as he did when he was younger. So Tom doesn't try to strike out every batter. Instead, he relies on his fielders to make the plays behind him.

300-Win Club

For a baseball pitcher, winning 300 games is the magical mark. Through 2006, only 22 pitchers in Major League history had won 300 games. Tom Glavine has his eye on joining that club. He went into the 2007 season with 290 career victories.

Tom is what baseball people call a "crafty" pitcher. He pitches the ball from one side of the plate to the other. He also moves the ball up and down in the **strike zone**. He mixes things up so the batter doesn't know where the ball is going next.

Another crafty left-hander is the New York Yankees' Andy Pettitte. Like Tom, Andy throws at different speeds and in different locations. Both Tom and Andy have the experience to win games even when they're not pitching their best.

Why "Southpaw"?

Left-handed pitchers are called southpaws because of the way baseball diamonds were first arranged. Years ago, diamonds were built so the batter would face east, instead of looking into the setting sun in the west. When the pitcher stood on the mound, he was facing west. That meant the pitcher's left hand— or "paw"—was on the south side.

Dontrelle Willis and Scott Kazmir are among the best up-and-coming southpaws in baseball.

Dontrelle, who pitches for the Florida Marlins, also is one of the most enjoyable pitchers to watch. He has a really high leg kick, then whips his fastball to the plate. His arms and legs seem to be going in different directions all at once. His motion makes it very hard for the batter to see the ball. Dontrelle was among the National League leaders in complete games and innings pitched in 2006.

The Devil Rays haven't been very good in recent years, but it's not because of Scott. As a 22-year-old in 2006, Scott won 10 games and made the AL All-Star team. He's already the leading strikeout pitcher in team history.

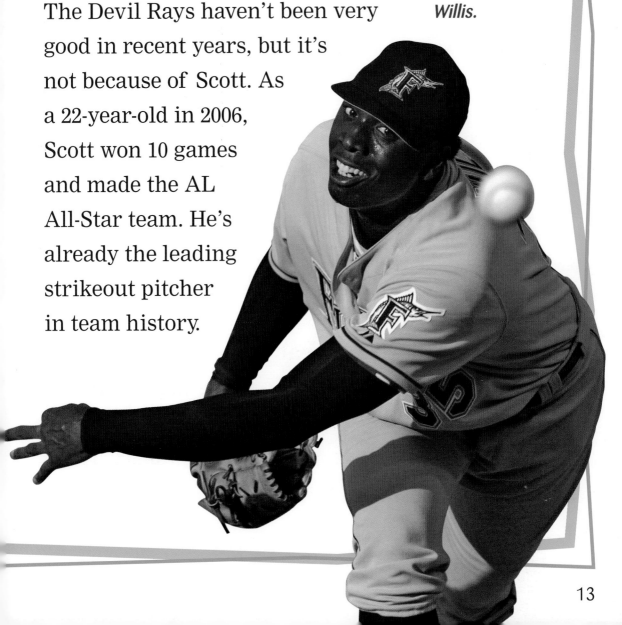

Here's a batter's-eye view of what it's like to face hard-throwing Dontrelle Willis.

13

2

THE

Righties

Today's baseball fans are lucky enough to watch two of the most dominating right-handed pitchers ever. The Mets' Pedro Martinez and the Astros' Roger Clemens probably will be in the Hall of Fame someday.

Pedro has been blowing away hitters since 1992. Batters were surprised that a pitcher who weighed only 180 pounds (82 kg) could generate such speed. Opposing hitters have batted just .209 against Pedro in his career. That's an average of only two hits for every 10 **at-bats**.

Roger was 44 years old in 2006, but he still struck out nearly one batter per inning and had an ERA of just 2.30. Roger wasn't sure if he was going to pitch again in 2007. There were a lot of Major League hitters hoping the man they call "The Rocket" was ready to retire!

Clemens's seven Cy Young Awards are the most in baseball history.

OPPOSITE PAGE Martinez has also pitched for the Dodgers, Expos, and Red Sox.

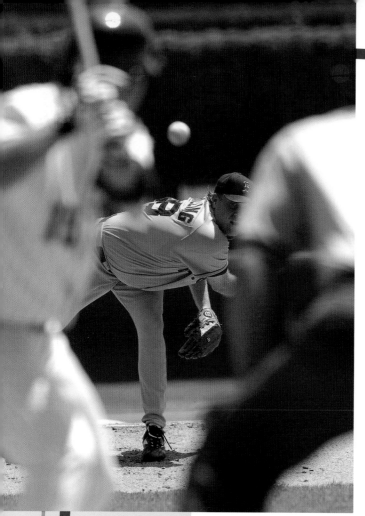

This batter is eyeing a fastball from Red Sox star Curt Schilling.

Boston's Curt Schilling is a right-handed pitcher who's strong and powerful. He relies on his 6-foot, 5-inch (196 cm), 235-pound (107 kg) body to muscle the ball past opposing batters.

Curt's a two-time champion, too. In 2001, he helped the Arizona Diamondbacks win the World Series. That year, he won 22 games and struck out 293 batters. In 2004, he won 21 games for the Boston Red Sox. He helped them win the World Series for the first time in 86 years!

Like Curt, the Braves' John Smoltz is still a hard thrower at an age most hurlers are considering retirement. Curt and John were both 39 years old during the 2006 season.

Smoltz joined the Braves in 1988. He won the Cy Young Award in 1996.

In 2005, John ranked third among all National League pitchers when he struck out 211 batters. He also spent a year as the Braves' **closer**. He helped Atlanta win 14 division titles, five NL **pennants**, and the 1995 World Series. John is a former Cy Young Award winner whose will to win has remained as strong as his fastball.

Which pitchers are following stars such as Clemens and Smoltz? In 2006, young Justin Verlander helped lead the Detroit Tigers to the American League pennant. Justin was just 23, but he showed great **poise**. He was among the AL's top 10 in wins (17) and ERA (3.63). In a big moment for a **rookie**, he started Game 1 of the World Series.

Verlander was a surprise success for the Tigers in 2006.

Josh Beckett knows what it's like to be a youngster on the World Series stage. He was only 23 when he and the Florida Marlins shut out the Yankees in the final game of the 2003 World Series. He now pitches for the Boston

Beckett is a great example of a "power pitcher," who tries to strike out batters.

Red Sox. Josh won 16 games for Boston in 2006.

Any big-league batter can hit a fastball that moves in a straight line, no matter how hard it's thrown. A fastball with lots of movement is the secret of Toronto ace Roy Halladay. Roy won 16 games for the Blue Jays in 2006. He ranked second in the AL with an ERA of 3.19.

With a 22–7 record, Halladay won the AL Cy Young Award in 2003.

Want more young talent? Jake Peavy, Roy Oswalt, and Carlos Zambrano might be the best young power pitchers in the National League. These players not only have a blazing fastball in common, but they also have strong wills to win. They won't back down from any hitter.

It's only 60 feet, 6 inches (18 m) from the pitcher's mound to home plate. Roy Oswalt of the Astros covers that distance with great skill.

Good Pitcher, Good Hitter

Most pitchers are poor hitters. But the Chicago Cubs' Carlos Zambrano doesn't fit the mold. In 2006, Zambrano hit six home runs. That tied the most in a season by a Cubs' pitcher.

Jake turned 25 during the 2006 season. He struck out 215 batters for the San Diego Padres. That was the second-best total in the NL. Carlos wasn't too far behind. He fanned 210 batters for the Cubs while winning 16 games for the second time in three seasons.

Roy won 15 games for the Astros in 2006. In his six years in the big leagues, he's had two seasons in which he's won 20 games and struck out more than 200 batters.

Webb grew up in Kentucky and joined the Diamondbacks in 2003.

You don't have to be a fastball pitcher to be a great Major League pitcher. The Diamondbacks' Brandon Webb was named the best pitcher in the NL in 2006. He won 16 games and had an ERA of 3.10. He tied for first in the NL in wins and shutouts, and tied for second in complete games and innings pitched. That all added up to Brandon's first Cy Young Award.

Brandon's best pitch is a **sinker**. It looks like a fastball, except it drops down suddenly as it reaches home plate. If the batter is lucky enough to hit the ball, it's most often hit into the ground.

Chris Carpenter won the NL Cy Young Award the season before Brandon. Chris won 21 games for the Cardinals in 2005. He doesn't have an overpowering fastball, but he has an excellent curveball. He can place his pitches exactly where he wants, too. He walks few opposing hitters.

Carpenter played for Toronto for six years before joining St. Louis in 2004.

In 2006, Chris ranked among the top 10 NL pitchers in wins, ERA, and strikeouts.

THE

Closers

All of the players we've met so far are starting pitchers. Sometimes, starting pitchers need a little help from their friends to win games—relief pitchers in the bullpen, that is. These days, the closer is the most important relief pitcher. That's the man whose job it is to get the final outs (or "close") a game in the ninth inning.

Perhaps one of the best closers of the 2000s is the Yankees' Mariano Rivera. His best pitch is a fastball that has lots of movement, especially right before the batter makes his swing. The pitch is sometimes called a "cutter." A cutter is especially hard for a batter to hit because it looks just like a regular fastball—until it's too late.

Rivera is the fourth player in history to **save** more than 400 games.

No player has saved more games in the World Series than the dependable Rivera.

Many young closers are power pitchers who try to blow their fastball by opposing hitters. Francisco Rodriguez, Billy Wagner, and B.J. Ryan are fireballing relievers who strike out at least one batter per inning.

Rodriguez and Wagner have fastballs clocked at more than 100 mph (161 kph). The hitter must decide whether to swing the bat in the blink of an eye! Of course, swinging the bat is one thing. Hitting the ball is another. Rodriguez struck out 98 batters in 73 innings while saving 47 games for the Angels in 2006. Wagner had 94 strikeouts in 72 innings while saving 40 games for the Mets.

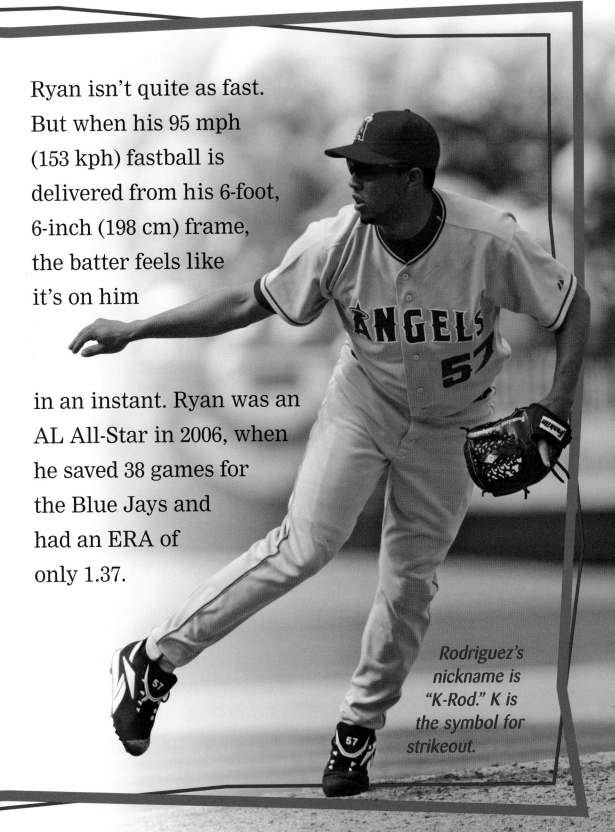

Ryan isn't quite as fast. But when his 95 mph (153 kph) fastball is delivered from his 6-foot, 6-inch (198 cm) frame, the batter feels like it's on him

in an instant. Ryan was an AL All-Star in 2006, when he saved 38 games for the Blue Jays and had an ERA of only 1.37.

Rodriguez's nickname is "K-Rod." K is the symbol for strikeout.

The Red Sox handed their closer's job to rookie Jonathan Papelbon in 2006. No problem. Papelbon saved 35 games and had a tiny ERA of 0.92. He was the second player ever with 35 saves and an ERA below 1.00.

Papelbon's greatest skill is his control. He rarely walks batters or allows hits.

Papelbon was a starting pitcher in the minor leagues before the Red Sox turned him into a closer. (Minor league teams are lower levels of **professional** ball, leading up to the Major Leagues.) His success as a closer has been a very pleasant surprise to Boston and its fans.

Japanese Import

The Dodgers' Takashi Saito entered his second Major League season in 2007. He wasn't new to baseball, though. Saito had been a star for many years in Japan. He was a rookie in the United States in 2006—but a 36-year-old rookie!

That won't happen with Huston Street. He's been a closer since college. With the A's, he saved 37 games in only his second season in 2006.

Street may be one of baseball's best closers for many years.

Today's top pitchers go to the mound in all shapes and sizes, and with different skills. They have something in common, though— they're all winners!

GLOSSARY

adapted   changed to fit a new situation

at-bat   any time a batter steps up to home plate to face a pitcher

changeup   a pitch that looks like a fastball, but is much slower

closer   a relief pitcher who comes in at the end of games in which his team is ahead

curveball   a pitch that changes direction slightly as it heads toward home plate

Cy Young Award   the trophy given each year to the best pitcher in the league. There is a separate award for both the American League and the National League each year

delivery   how a pitcher throws the ball to the plate

ERA   earned run average—a number that shows how many runs a pitcher allows every nine innings.

pennants   nickname for league or division championships

poise   the ability to do or play well, even in difficult situations

professional   a person paid to perform an activity

rookie   a player in his first season

save   when a pitcher comes into a close game and finishes off a victory for his team

sinker   a pitch that drops sharply as it reaches home plate

strike zone   the area above home plate between a batter's knees and shoulders; balls pitched into this area are called strikes

FIND OUT MORE

BOOKS

Johan Santana (Amazing Athletes)
by Jeffrey Zuehlke (First Avenue Editions, 2007)
A young reader's profile of the Minnesota Twins' superstar pitcher.

On the Mound With Randy Johnson
by Matt Christopher (Little, Brown Young Readers, 2003)
A look at what made Randy Johnson one of baseball's great pitchers.

Who is Baseball's Greatest Pitcher?
by Jeff Kisseloff (Cricket Books, 2003)
An information-packed book that covers more than 30 of the best pitchers in baseball.

WEB SITES

Visit our Web page for lots of links about baseball pitchers:
www.childsworld.com/links

Note to Parents, Teachers, and Librarians: We routinely check our Web links to make sure they're safe, active sites—so encourage your readers to check them out!

INDEX

JIM GIGLIOTTI is a freelance writer who lives in southern California with his wife and two children. He has written more than two dozen books on sports and personalities, including a book on Michelle Wie for Child's World's "World's Greatest Athletes" series.